THE WORST CLASS IN SCHOOL

Poems collected by Brian Moses

Illustrations by Kelly Waldek

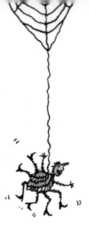

Wayland Paperback Poetry

The Upside Down Frown Collected by Andrew Fusek Peters

The Worst Class In School Collected by Brian Moses

THE WORST CLASS IN SCHOOL

First published in 1999 by
Wayland (Publishers) Ltd
61 Western Rd, Hove
East Sussex BN3 1JD, England
www.wayland.co.uk
This collection © Wayland Publishers Ltd 1999

Commissioning Editor: Paul Mason
Production Controller: Carol Titchener
Designer/typesetter: Danny McBride

British Library Cataloguing in Publication Data is available for this title.

ISBN 0 7502 2540 8

Printed in Hong Kong by Wing King Tong.

CONTENTS

THE WORST CLASS IN THE SCHOOL

Brian Moses

We're the worst class in the school
and we know it,
we're the worst class in the school
and we show it. . .
We frighten the teachers and the governors,
we frighten the visiting inspectors,
We're the worst class in the school
and they know it!

And of course they all think
that they can defeat us,
reach the unreachable,
teach the unteachable,
but we know better,
no one can beat us.

We're the worst class in the school,
so come and meet us. . .

5

WHO'S WHO IN THE WORST CLASS?

Brian Moses

First of all there's my mate Selina,
she makes more noise than a vacuum cleaner,
screams and yells at very high pitch,
wish we could fit her with an on/off switch.
There's Liam who is far too handy with his fist
and Grace whose knickers are always in a twist.
There's Joe who brings yucky things to school
but his pet tarantula is really cool!
There's Chloe and Zoe who can't sit still
and Michael whose habits make us all feel ill.
There's a quick tempered girl whose name is Shannon
who explodes with a ROAR just like a cannon.

There's Shakira and Mira who can't stop yakking
and a kid called Bruce whose senses are lacking,
he really shouldn't be out on the loose,
once he gelled his hair with Strawberry mousse!
There's Karen and Sharon who flirt with the boys
and everything Faith does always annoys.
We think she must wash in her mum's perfume
there's a sickly smell all around our room.
There's a lad called Lloyd who thinks it's funny
to hop around and speak like Bugs Bunny.
But nobody laughs, we all think it's sad
and the teachers agree that he must be mad.

scary

karen

Sharon

bounce

bounce

Lloyd

Then there's Hannah and Rick who go out with each other
and Leroy who's even worse than his brother.
They once brought a pack of soapflakes to school
and emptied it all into our swimming pool!
There's Conan who thinks he's a tough little fighter
and Kelly, when cornered, is known as a biter.
There's Hetty who seems to think she's better
than all of us, so sometimes we get her,
and Felicity threatens to twist her ears,
till we chase her home and it ends in tears.

And there's Malik and Joel, Mohammed and Lee,
Celine, Marisa and finally me.....

We're the worst class in the school
and the worst class RULE........OK?

Hetty. Ha Ha.

Me
(at school)

prison!!

MO'S RAP

James Carter

I'm Mohammed - you can call me 'Mo'
Gimme high five - wicked - yo!
Now check this out from brother Mo
Gonna tell you some stuff that you ought to know
I'm doin' this rap, to set things straight
As people been dissin' me n' my mates
Folks been sayin' our class ain't good
But people don't see we're misunderstood
If you want the truth you need the facts
To know where things are really at
You'll soon agree we done nothin' wrong
If you check out the words to this song

You know 'bout Leroy, his brother and the pool -
And all those bubbles? Well, they ain't fools
They bought soapflakes to wash their clothes
But the box disappeared - how? Who knows?
It turned up by the pool as the Head went by -
The Head tripped up, the box took a dive -
The Head had to find some kids to blame
And written on the box was Leroy's name
Leroy and his bro' - they got it in the neck
'You've done it this time' said the Head

Hey people - listen to me!
Try and see things from my P.O.V.!
My P.O.V. - my Point Of View
For kids have got opinions too
give us R.E.S.P.E.C.T.
Respect for all my mates n' me

8

I'm up here on the mic
to tell you what it's like
I hope you're buyin'
'Cos Mo ain't lyin'

And next time that you hear about us
Stop and think about the fuss
That people make and what is right
For teachers say whatever they like
And we don't even need to get caught
As teachers are always finding fault
So spare some thought n' sympathy
For Mo, Joe, Zoe and Chloe
Mira, Shakira, Hetty and Kelly
Karen, Sharon, Liam and Lee
And try and see things from our P.O.V.

You see this class ? It ain't that bad –
It ain't *bad* – it's *wicked* man!
My rap is done – gonna wrap it up now –
So it's yo from Mo – chill out, ciao!

FAITHFUL

Philip Waddell

Faith brings Sir stuff
(A cup cake, a fruit pie)
Last Christmas she gave him
A sort of a tie.
(Knitted it myself Sir!)

Faith sits at the front
Doused in perfume that reeks
Sniv'lling 'Sir can't be heard
If everyone speaks.'
(Pay attention you lot!)

Faith hangs on Sir's words
And her cheeks flush bright red
If ever we tease
'Guess who Faith's going to wed?'
(You're all so immature!)

Faith's faithful to Sir
'It's the least Sir deserves'
And our whole class agrees
THAT FAITH GETS
          ON OUR NERVES!
(Sir's asked you not to shout!)

Roger Stevens

When our class lines up
It's a perfect line
Except for Selina!

When we walk to the hall
We are as quiet as mice
Except for Selina!

When we have silent reading
You can hear a pin drop
And you can hear Selina!

Teacher says he has no favourites.
He says we are *all* his favourites.
Except for Selina!

He likes her best!

LEROY

Dave Ward

Leroy's mother
says Leroy
is even worse than his brother.

Leroy's brother
would take half an hour
to walk ten minutes to school:
But Leroy will wander right out of the gate
and never get there at all.

Leroy's brother
would fall asleep
in the middle of three times seven
and wake up to find the answer was 311:
but Leroy will fall asleep
in the middle of Hadrian's Wall -
and if they don't shake him at break time,
he'll never wake up at all.

Leroy's brother
would spend all morning
tugging the girl-in-front's hair:
but Leroy will take Chloe's pony tail
and tie it onto her chair.

Leroy's brother
would spend school dinners
firing off pellets of peas:
but Leroy can clear the lunch hall
with one brain-damaging sneeze.

Leroy's brother
would bring his pet spiders
to let loose at the back of the room:
but Leroy unfastens his basket of snakes
and everyone has to go home.

Leroy's mother
says Leroy
is even worse than his brother.

Leroy's brother
would get back home
and give his Mum a great big kiss:
but Leroy will give her
one, two and three -
and another one for his sis.

And Leroy's smiles
are miles and miles
wider than his brother's.
- But I couldn't have one without the other -
so says Leroy's mother.

13

THE DUET

Trevor Harvey

Lloyd and Joel do armpits.
They do them night and day.
They do them when the teacher's near -
And when he walks away.
They do them at the swimming pool.
They do them in P.E.
They do them when they're in the park
And while they watch T.V.
They've found that doing armpits
Makes adults go BRIGHT RED!
And when Lloyd stays at Joel's house,
They practise them in bed.
They're really VERY musical -
They make a little tune.
They're working out if there's a way
To bounce them off the Moon -
Then EVERYONE could hear them!

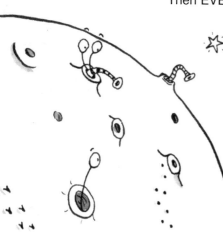

Frances Nagle

I'm not the eldest.
If I was I'd show 'em
Who's the boss,
Just like our Ross.

And I'm not the next,
'Cos three of them do work (for the D.S.S.).
Then there's Justine and Norm
In a higher form.

I'm not the baby,
Obviously.
And I'm not the twins
Who're both younger than me.

So's Patrick whose nose
Drips pints of snot.
He thinks he's cleverer than me.
I bash him a lot.

I must be in the middle of this muddle –
Sixth or seventh,
Fifth or eighth,
Or thereabouts.

There's eleven of us
All together.
Where am I?
Can you sort it out?

15

THERE ARE TWO SIDES TO MICHAEL

Philip Waddell

There are two sides to Michael
The first side is this –
Messy and horrid
But that one is bliss
Compared to the other...
The other's much worse!
It's when he's in love
And writes soppy verse.

Yuuuukkkk!!!!

The love poems:

Monday

To Sharon

Sharon I luv you
Sharon yore dear
Sharon Ime shivery
When you are near.
Sharon Ide wash for you
Give me some hope
Just say the word
Ive got money for soap!

Yores eternully,
Mikey xxxx

16

Tuesday

To Michael

Dear Michael, I'm touched
That you'd wash just for me
But pledged to another
Alas, I'm not free.

So sorry am I
Not to give you some hope,
Your verse I'm returning
But do buy the soap!

Regards,

Sharon

Karen

Wednesday
~~Monday~~

To ~~Sharon~~
Karen
~~Sharon~~ I luv you
Karen
~~Sharon~~ yore dear
Karen
~~Sharon~~ Ime shivery
When you are near.

Karen
~~Sharon~~ Ide wash for you
Give me some hope
Just say the word
Ive got money for soap!

Yores eternully,
Mikey xxxx

TRUE CONFESSIONS RICK 4 HANNAH

Mike Johnson

Next to waiting to weigh whales at a Whale Weigh Station,
I like you best

and,
next to lunching on the largest ever leaning tower of pizza,
I like you best

and,
next to looking at my **All-Colour Wonder Wildlife Book's**:
lively leaf-cutter ants
languid lungfish
likeable lemurs
lickety-split lar gibbons
and
illogical llamas,
I like you best

and,
next to wearing virtual wellies, on cyber-strolls with wildebeest,
I like you best

and,
next to me, especially (as the sun sets in the West),
I like you best.

THE TEACHER'S MONDAY MORNING THOUGHTS

John Coldwell

What did I do?

What did I do?

To deserve horrible pupils

Like you, you and you.

What can I say?

What can I say?

I'd be so very happy

With you all away.

When will it end?

When will it end?

Oh, for two days of school and a

Five day weekend.

I can't stand the tension

I can't stand the tension

Will I live long enough to

Collect my pension?

THE CARETAKER'S COMPLAINTS

Trevor Harvey

I KNOW ALL THEIR NAMES –
The sly and the cunning,
The ones you can't trust –
'SELINA! STOP RUNNING!'
Joel, who's forever
Blowing his nose,
Leaving used tissues
Wherever he goes;
Michael, who's sick
In 'unusual' places
(Under the piano
And in teachers' cases);
Rick, whose graffiti
Adorns every door;
Malik, whose boots
Always scratch my hall floor;
Marisa, who seemed
To behave *really* well –
'Til she raided the Tuck Shop
And gave the staff HELL!

These kids just spell Trouble!
The staff are the same –
They spend HOURS drinking tea,
Which gives 'work' a bad name!
THUMB TACKS get used –
They're ALL OVER the place!
Making holes in my walls –
It's a flippin' DISGRACE!
Why on earth they should ever
WANT to display
This EVIL LOT'S work
I really can't say!
I'd ban kids from school –
I'd ban teachers, too –
Were it left up to me,
Yes, that's just what I'd do!
Then a caretaker's job
Might become more delightful. . .
'PUT THAT VISITOR DOWN, LLOYD –
AND STOP BEING SPITEFUL!'

THE WORST CLASS MUSEUM VISIT

Marian Swinger

The museum attendant moans, 'Not them again.
'Orrible kids they are, each one a pain.'
We pour in. Our teacher is dragging his feet.
His 'Behave yourself, Conan' comes out as a bleat.
We make for the mummies, and, just as we feared,
Leroy and his brother have both disappeared
to leap forth wrapped in bandages, like a bad dream.
Our teacher, unnerved, stumbles back with a scream
Then, off to the dinosaurs, 'Bruce! Don't touch that!'
A skeleton collapses. 'You vandal! You brat!'
the museum attendant howls. 'Get out of here.
Look at the mess you've made. Bones everywhere.'
Then Joe shouts, 'Look! Spiders! Inside a glass case.'
But Selina has got a strange look on her face.
'I DON'T LIKE SPIDERS.' she bawls at the class.
The shrill shrieks surround us and shatter the glass.

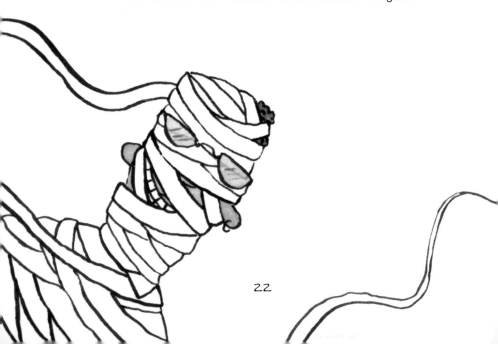

'Where's Faith?' says our teacher. We hunt round the room
sniffing the air till a waft of perfume
leads us as far as the china display
where Kelly bites Lloyd when he gets in her way
(he's moving, as usual, with rabbit-like hops)
and he leaps, in his agony over the top
of a giant Chinese vase, slips, and falls in head first.
The museum attendant roars, 'You are the worst
class that's ever polluted this place.'
We're escorted straight back to the coach in disgrace
by a grim faced security guard with a cosh.
He menaces teacher, who quavers, 'Oh gosh.'
Near home, in a traffic jam, hemmed in by cars,
we realise we've left Lloyd behind, in the vase.

BUGS BUNNY AND THE CLEANING LADY

Clare Bevan

The museum was musty
And cold as a tomb
As I stomped past the kids
With my mop and my broom
To clear up the floor
Of the Dinosaur Room.

I flicked with my cloth,
I wiped and I swept,
But the rubbish and mud –
Well, a saint would have wept.
There were left-over lunches
Wherever I stepped.

I was boiling with rage,
I was fit for a fight,
When a boy stumbled in
With his coat buttoned tight.
He blinked like a rabbit
Afraid I would bite.

'I've come for my hat.'
His voice was a bleat,
He shuffled and shivered
And stared at his feet.
The most terrified child
That you ever could meet.

But I glared at his face
And his strange, flappy ears,
I pointed at crisp bags,
I worked on his fears -
Why should I care
If he burst into tears?

'You're one of the vandals
Who came here today!
Would you do this at home?'
I ranted away.
'If your Mum saw this mess
Do you know what she'd say?'

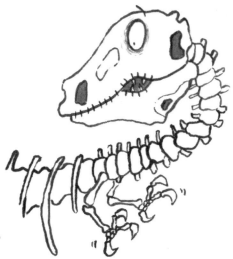

The boy twitched his nose,
He hopped like a flea,
His rabbity eyes
Were as sad as could be.
He whispered, 'My Mum
never notices me.'

I found him his hat,
Pulled it over his head,
'Get back to your teacher.
Clear off now,' I said.
But I wanted to say
Something kinder instead.

I finished the job,
And I switched off the light,
I grumbled my way
Through the wild, winter night.
But that rabbity boy –
Well, I hope he's all right.

THE CLASS NEXT DOOR

Frances Nagle

One thing's for certain, one thing's for sure,
We hate the goody-goodies in the class next door.

They suck up to their teacher and obey the law.
We despise the creeps in the class next door.

We capture them at playtime and pin them to the floor,
The feeble goody-goodies in the class next door.

They tell on us – that's something we all deplore,
So we beat up any narks in the class next door.

One made it up I'd punched him in the jaw.
They're a bunch of liars in the class next door.

My dad says he'll be up to give 'em what-for,
Those blank blank trouble-makers in the class next door.

Sir says he wishes that we were more
Like the little angels in the class next door.

We say 'You don't Sir, it'd be a bore
If we were goody-goodies like the class next door.'

He says 'I'm not so sure.'

27

CORRIDOR

Dave Calder

4B

I'm standing in the corridor
with my back against the wall
just outside the classroom door,
I don't like being here at all,
shuffling, muttering it isn't fair
all I did
was pull Sharon's hair

It's lonely out here, it's boring
away from my pal's silly grin,
and I want to hear the story -
perhaps I could sneak back in
and anyway, it isn't fair
all I did
was push Rick off his chair

How long is this going to last?
What are they laughing at now?
What if the head should come past
and give me an awful row?
I keep telling myself I don't care
it's not right, it isn't fair
all I did
was throw Joe's book in the air
push Rick off his chair
pull Sharon's hair
and swear

At our school,
our class,
every day and without fail
- so it seems -
gets letters to take home.
'Very important,' says teacher!

The letters arrive from the office
looking ever so neat and impressive,
typed out on the school's new word processor,
and in all sorts of different colours!
Then at the end of the day
they are usually handed out in a rush
for we're all scrambling to get out
and teacher's forgotten them.
Finally, when we are released,
we rush out of the classroom
school bag in one hand - letter in the other
but once outside then the fun begins:

For Liam makes aeroplanes with them,
Chloe and Zoe draw on them,
Lloyd practises origami on them,
Shakira and Mira lob them in the bushes,
or at each other.
Mohammed sucks them,
Lee chucks them,
Bruce bites on them,
Faith writes on them,
while Leroy chews them
and then screws them up
to play football with **BUT**
the one thing our class doesn't ever do is
read them!

29

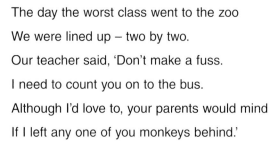

THE CLASS VISIT TO THE ZOO

John Coldwell

The day the worst class went to the zoo
We were lined up – two by two.
Our teacher said, 'Don't make a fuss.
I need to count you on to the bus.
Although I'd love to, your parents would mind
If I left any one of you monkeys behind.'

Joe arrived late and was lumbered with Grace.
'Oh no,' he said, 'I can't stand her face.
If you think I'm walking hand in hand with her,
Then you've got another think coming, Sir!'
The teacher said, 'It's just for the day.
She's your partner at the zoo. O.K.'

At the end of the day we piled back in the bus
And Sir counted to check he'd got all of us.
Hannah and Rick appeared to be missing
But we found them on the back seat, hugging and kissing
'Good,' said Sir. 'Now let's head for school
Before you lot drive me up the wall.'

Half way home Selina, cried, 'Oh no!
Can we stop the bus because I need to go.'
Sir said, 'We haven't got time for the loo.'
But a voice near the front grunted, 'Ooh, Ooh, Ooh.'
The teacher's jaw dropped like a trap.
'Joe! There's a monkey sitting on your lap.

'Tell me, where is Grace!' cried Sir in a rage.
Joe said, 'Oh she's safe in the monkey cage.
I didn't like Grace and she didn't like me
So I swopped her for this chimpanzee.'
'Oh dear,' cried Sir, 'This can't be true.
Driver turn round. It's back to the zoo.'

When we got the zoo, the keeper was waiting.
He exchanged Grace for the ape - no hesitating.
Joe and the chimp waved goodbye for a while
Until Malik started chanting, rapper style,
'Grace! Grace! Belongs in the zoo.
The chimp was better looking than you.'

AT THE ZOO

Dave Calder

The lions have dug deep burrows,
the snakes have coiled up in despair,
the crocodile has lost his smile,
the rhino is running scared.

The hippos are wearing crash helmets,
the camels have clumped off to grump,
the leopard is looking rather sick
his spots have changed to goosebumps.

The panther's turned pale with fear,
as white as the arctic fox,
the elephants are trying hard
to disguise themselves as rocks.

32

The turtles are sheltering in their shells,
the seals have submerged out of sight,
the giraffes are giggling nervously,
the tigers tremble with fright.

The birds of prey are praying today,
they've disappeared to the last feather,
all you can hear from the herd of red deer
is knobbly knees knocking together.

The keepers are locked in their office,
only one brave cockatoo
shrieks out a final warning:
6D have arrived at the zoo!

33

THE SCHOOL PHOTOGRAPH

Bernard Young

What a picture!

A <u>silent</u> Selina!
A grimacing Grace.
(Joe's dangling a furry thing
in front of her face).

Liam and Conan are exchanging blows.
Michael's got a finger stuck right up his nose.

Daft Bruce has adopted a very strange pose
and is wearing his weirdest of weirdest of clothes.

Kelly looks to be snarling. She's baring her teeth.
(Some of the things we get up to you just wouldn't believe).

There's a fierce-looking Shannon.
Faith, with a sneer.
Lloyd is a-leaping.
Zoe and Chloe, a blur.

Shakira and Mira are mid-word, open mouthed.
Karen and Sharon are attempting to pout.

Hannah and Rick are, of course, kissing.
There's no sign of Leroy. He <u>appears</u> to be missing.

Hetty, as usual, has her nose in the air.
Felicity's behind her, reaching out for her ears.

And there's Malik and Joel, Mohammed and Lee,
Celine, Marisa and finally me
pulling rude faces,
having a laugh,
all captured forever on the school photograph.

MR MCKAY'S DREAM

Clive Webster

'The golden rule is to count them on
So you know how many you've got,
And then when it's time for coming back home
You'll be sure that you've got the whole lot.'

So said the Head to Mr McKay
When he took the worst class to France.
But Mr McKay had other ideas –
For this was his one golden chance.

He'd waited for months for something like this,
And he said, 'I'll count 'em all right,
But not for the reason that you say I should.'
And he chuckled in secret delight.

He wanted to know how many there were,
Right down to the last dreadful one,
Because when he heaved them all overboard
He needed to know they'd all gone!

WELL, IT'S A THOUGHT

The teacher asked in English one day,
'Complete the saying which goes,
"A bird in the hand. . ."' and Michael replied,
'Makes it harder to blow your nose.'

WELL, SORT OF. . .

'Why were you absent yesterday?'
Leroy was asked by the Head.
'I was sick sir, really sick sir,'
Leroy immediately said.

'So why is it you're always sick
When United play at home?'
'Well sir, the way United play
Would make anyone sick,' Leroy moaned.

37

WELCOME TO OUR PET'S DAY

Clare Bevan

Our teacher must be round the bend
Or else a total fool
To organise a Pets Day for
The Worst Class In The School!

Michael (who's disgusting)
Brought a carton, brightly draped.
A GENUINE flea circus. . .
Until the fleas escaped.
Shannon, looking moody,
Arrived with Rambo Rat.
She said he wouldn't bite us
(And our teacher fell for that!)

Mira and Shakira brought
A Mynah bird who talks.
Bruce trooped in with Goldie –
A fish he takes for walks.
Conan brought The Mauler,
A tom-cat with one ear
Who swallowed Hannah's love bird,
Then Rick's as well – oh dear!

Grace brought thirteen guinea pigs
Who scampered round the room.
Hetty brought her pony
Plus a bucket and a broom.
Felicity's fat lizard
Gave the pony such a fright
Hetty had to clean the floor –
It took her half the night.

Lloyd, of course, brought Bugsy
A rabbit with sad eyes.
Leroy brought a six-foot snake,
(A hose pipe in disguise!)
Joe, you must have guessed it,
Brought a spider huge and hairy,
When we saw her fangs we screamed,
But let's be fair – she's SCARY !

As for me, I'm not allowed
An animal – and yet
I brought along a Dinosaur.
(He's my Computer Pet.)
Everyone brought SOMETHING
And showed it round with pride,
I can't think why our teacher
Had to run away and hide.

We did our best to please him
We followed every rule
When he organised a Pets Day for
The Worst Class In The School.

39

PARENT'S EVENING

Barry Buckingham

It's Parents' Evening, and in off the street
come the mums and dads for a chance to meet
the masters and mistresses teaching their kids
about sums, punctuation and the Pyramids.
But here, in the school's worst pupils' room,
the heart of the teacher is filled with gloom.
Just one quick glance, and he's given up hope.
These mums and dads won't help him cope.

There's Sharon's pa in a naff string vest
with hairs sticking through it from his uncombed chest,
and Rick's dad grinning as he watches his wife
initialing a desk with her army knife.
Then Lee's baby sister is yelling for a feed,
wriggling about like a centipede,
staring with envy and dribbling lips
at Felicity's dad eating haddock and chips.

The dolly-bird mum of Marisa is there
with long green finger-nails, glitter in her hair,
rings through her nostrils, chains in her ears,
bright blue lipstick and two canned beers.
And Faith would have felt really proud of her mum,
blowing such whoppers with her bubble-gum,
while everyone's frowning at Leroy's ma
as she goes around puffing on a huge cigar.

Michael's mum has a dose of the 'flu.
Big red nose, and the rest of her blue.
And Kelly's dad's on his mobile 'phone.
Loud voice, and a laugh like a bent trombone.
In isolation, in a corner of the room,
sits Hetty's mother, stiff as a broom,
nose in the air, all la-di-da!
surrounded by smoke from that foul cigar.

Then suddenly people are starting to cough,
and the classroom smoke alarm goes off.
The whole room empties in five seconds flat
(No pupils could clear it as fast as that!)
leaving the teacher slumped on the floor
and too fazed out to get to the door.

And where are the parents who didn't turn up?
At home watching telly. . . UEFA Cup!

THE DAY THE INSPECTORS CAME

David Harmer

The first Inspector walked into the room
as Art was starting for the day
he bellowed out in a voice of doom
'Your teacher's missing, has he run away?'
That's when Leroy threw the blue paint
and Michael started to eat the clay.

The next Inspector rushed through the door
tripped over the glue pot Mohammed threw
at Leroy who was mixing loads more
bright coloured paint bombs in Hetty's shoe
the first Inspector drooped in a faint
the other one's foot stuck to the floor.

42

The third Inspector raced to the scene
as Bruce and Joe were just finding out
if their pet rats looked good painted green
dropped one on Selina to make her shout
all of us now were horribly mucky
the best messed up lesson there'd ever been!

The corner cupboard started to shake
and our teacher fell out looking rather upset
we'd locked him in there just before break
all this excitement had made us forget
'Painting?' he asked 'You Inspectors are plucky
taking this lot for Art can be a mistake.'

43

THE INSPECTOR'S REPORT

David Hamer

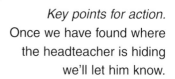

Strengths of the school.
The tiles in the entrance hall are very shiny
all the footballs in the PE store were full of air
on Tuesday we saw a dinner lady smile.
The white lines on the yard are straight
except when they are supposed to be curvy
the paints in the cupboards are very colourful
and the glue in the glue pots is very sticky.

Weaknesses of the school.
Year Three, Year Four, Year Five and Year Six
know very little
English, science or mathematics
also they appear to be entirely ignorant of Music
Geography, History, Technology
PE, RE and ICT
though the little so and so's
achieve very high standards
in tricks with yo-yos.

Year Six.
These really are
the worst class we have ever seen!
We mean EVER.
In the entire WORLD.
Their teacher agrees
he's just resigned!

Key points for action.
Once we have found where
the headteacher is hiding
we'll let him know.

44

Marian Swinger

Dear Head,

I've gone. I've had enough. If you don't like it, well, that's tough.
They went too far today, that's all. I've got my pride. No, I won't crawl.
I've seen my lawyer. I may sue. They smeared my chair with superglue
then snatched my toupee. Just my luck, I tried to apprehend them. Stuck,
glued cement-like to my chair, with splinters in my derriere,
I writhed in anguish of the soul while glimpsing outside, up the pole,
(you know, the one that flies the flag) my toupee, fluttering like a rag
and no one came although I called. I hobbled to the staffroom, bald.
I want revenge. I'll make them pay. I penned this missive just to say
I'd rather be a tax inspector, fast food waiter, rubbish collector,
lion tamer, tramp, or preacher, anything, but not a teacher,

Farewell for ever, dearest Head. Employ a riot cop instead.

45

MISS HONEY

Brian Moses

When we first discovered Miss Honey
was to be our new Year Six teacher,
we gaped, mouths open, stopped in our tracks
at the sight of this heaven-sent creature.

She was trim, she was neat, she was lovely,
and less than a hundred years old.
She was every fairytale princess
with a smile like liquid gold.

Most of the boys lost their hearts
and would have died for her then and there,
captivated by the pull of her eyes
and the way she flicked back her hair.

They were hooked from the very first moment
she asked them to do her a favour,
they were knights of King Arthur's Round Table
with courage that would never waver.

She wafted between the tables
like a model more used to the catwalk,
while her voice was like honey itself
and we'd much rather listen than talk.

She was wonderful, she was gorgeous,
she was Beauty and we'd been such beasts,
but Miss Honey tamed the wildest class
and all resistance ceased.

Brian Moses

Well, what do you think,
what do you know,
all in all
it just goes to show...

The class that once
drove everyone bats,
all scored Level 5
in the Year 6 SATS.

All except me,
that is....
I got 6
and a kiss

from miss!

MORE POETRY FROM WAYLAND

Wayland Poetry Collection:

Themed collections by Brian Moses, illustrated by Kelly Waldek
27 x 22 cm, full-colour,
32 pages: £9.99 hardback and £4.99 paperback

Poems About Animals	0 7502 2437 1 hbk, 0 7502 2441 X pbk
Poems About Food	0 7502 2438 X hbk, 0 7502 2442 8 pbk
Poems About Space	0 7502 2436 3 hbk, 0 7502 2240 1 pbk
Poems About School	0 7502 2435 5 hbk, 0 7502 2439 8 pbk

Poems About Me/Poems About You and Me:

Poetry about what it means to be a member of society.
27 x 22 cm, full-colour, 32 pages, : £9.50 hbk & £4.99 paperback

ALSO AVAILABLE AS BIG BOOKS AND IN EDUCATIONAL PACKS

Big Books 44 x 36 cm, available at £13.99

Poems About You and Me	0 7502 1128 8 hbk, 0 7502 2384 7 pbk, 0 7502 2386 3 BB
Poems About Me	0 7502 1127 X hbk, 0 7502 2383 9 pbk, 07502 26781 BB

The Upside Down Frown: Shape poems

A5, black-and-white illustrations by Mike Flanagan. Andrew Fusek Peters has
collected poems that will make you think again about poetry, featuring worms that
actually turn, a girl who sneezes mushy peas, and many more weirdnesses besides.

The Upside Down Frown	0 7502 2596 3 pbk: £3.99, 48 pages

Poems About:

Themed collections of poems for primary children.
27 x 22 cmm full-colour, £4.99 paperback only.

Poems About Families	0 7502 2397 9
Poems About Feelings	0 7502 1936 X
Poems About Journeys	0 7502 1931 9
Poems About Weather	0 7502 1930 0

TO ORDER

Contact Wayland's Customer
Services Department on:
01273 722 561,

or write to them at:
61 Western Rd, Hove,
East Sussex BN3 1JD.